Are...
Handsome?

For Tania Ramos

First published in Great Britain in 2007
by Zero To Ten Limited,
part of the Evans Publishing Group
2A Portman Mansions, Chiltern Street,
London W1U 6NR

Text and illustrations copyright © 2006 l' ecole des loisirs
Translation copyright © 2007 Zero To Ten Limited
Originally published as 'C'est Moi le Plus Beau'
by Pastel, an imprint of l'ecole des loisirs © 2006

A CIP catalogue record for this book is available
from the British Library

ISBN 978 184089 5056

Printed in Italy

Mario Ramos

Aren't I
Handsome?

ZERO TO TEN

After breakfast the wolf puts on
his favourite piece of clothing.
  'Mmm! I'm ravishing! I think I'll go
for a little walk so everyone can
admire me!'

He passes Little Red Riding Hood.

'Oh what a pretty little outfit! Tell me, little strawberry, who is the most handsome, you or I?' asks the wolf.

'The most handsome … is you, Mister Wolf,' replies Little Red Riding Hood.

'There, you see? Children always
see the truth. I *am* the most charming
animal of all,' trumpets the wolf.

Then he meets the Three Little Pigs.
'Hey, little ones! Taking a trot in the
woods? Tell me, puffing piglets,'
demands the wolf, 'who is the most
handsome animal?'

'Oh you are ... you are marvellous,
you shine like a thousand stars,' reply
the three little pigs, shaking.

'Heh, heh! I shine and I dazzle,
I am resplendent and I radiate.
I light up the woods with my looks –
I am simply a marvel!' boasts the
jubilant wolf.

Then he meets the Seven Dwarfs.

'Ho ho! You all look dreadful. You should think about taking a rest. Now then,' asks the wolf, 'do you know – which of us is the most handsome?'

'Er, the most handsome … is … is you, big wolf,' chorus the little men.

'Tra-la-la! I am the star of the
woods,' sings the wolf.
'I am on top form today.'

Next he meets Snow White.

'Ooh la la! How pale you are. You don't look well, my child. You should look after yourself. Now then, look carefully and tell me: who is the most handsome creature in the woods?'

'Well ... er ... it's you, definitely you,' replies the little girl, nervously.

'Ho ho. Yes of course! Good answer,
little one! I am the king of these woods.
I am the most beautiful of all!
Everyone adores me!' shouts the wolf.

Then the wolf meets the little dragon.

'Oh, hello. What a surprise. Are your mummy and daddy with you?' checks the wolf, looking around.

'No, my parents are at home,' says the little dragon.

'Ah ha, perfect, perfect! Tell me, ridiculous little gherkin,' continues the wolf, 'who is the most handsome beast that you know?'

'The most handsome is my daddy, and he is the one who taught me how to breathe fire!'

'Now stop asking me
your silly questions and
go away! I'm playing
hide and seek with bird,'
says the little dragon.